the Cat

Colin and
Jacqui Hawkins

KINDERSLEY
York • Stuttgart

Do you know Pat the cat?

C

Hi!

He's very fat.

f

Fat?
I'm not
fat!

He wears a top hat
when he sits on his mat.

m
I do like my hat.

But look! Who's that in Pat's hat?

h
Who's that in my hat?

It's Tat the bat

b
Hello, Pat.
Tat
A bat?
In a hat?

and Nat the rat.

r

Bad Nat, get out of my hat!
Hello, Pat.
Nat
A rat in a hat?
Well, fancy that.

Pat is too fat to get Nat out of his hat.

So that's where he sat.

While Pat sat, out popped Nat.

N
What a clever rat.

Now there's a hole in the ha
of the cat called Pat.

Pat

A DORLING KINDERSLEY BOOK

Published in the United Kingdom in 1995
by Dorling Kindersley Limited,
9 Henrietta Street, London WC2E 8PS
Reprinted 1996
Published in the United States in 1995
by Dorling Kindersley Publishing, Inc.,
95 Madison Avenue, New York, New York 10016

4 6 8 10 9 7 5 3

ISBN 0-7513-5352-3 (UK)
ISBN 0-7894-0154-1 (US)

Reproduction by DOT Gradations
Printed in Italy by L.E.G.O.